A Gilded Christmas

J. Curtis Smith

A Gilded Christmas

J. Curtis Smith

WestBow
PRESS
A DIVISION OF THOMAS NELSON

ISBN: 978-1-4497-7491-2 (sc)
ISBN: 978-1-4497-7492-9 (e)

Library of Congress Control Number: 2012921294

WestBow Press books may be ordered through booksellers or by contacting:

WestBow Press
A Division of Thomas Nelson
1663 Liberty Drive
Bloomington, IN 47403
www.westbowpress.com
1-(866) 928-1240

Printed in the United States of America

WestBow Press rev. date: 11/09/2012

This book is
Presented as a gift

To: _____

From: _____

Personal Acknowledgments

I would like to thank God, and my fiancée Toni Berry for all her hard work and patients. Also I would like to thank my two children, Austin Smith and Allison Smith. I love each of you.

The last painting in the book was commissioned by Sheila Kinsey a renowned Santa artist, from Dallas Texas. The oil painting features all the images that we perceive on Christmas Eve. Very few of us have ever seen the jolly old elf, because we should all be fast asleep on Christmas Eve. Thank you Sheila!

CHRISTMAS DINNER BEHIND THE SCENES

CHRISTMAS WAITS

THE CHRISTMAS SEASON IN THE SHOPPING DISTRICT.

NEW YORK'S ORIGINAL RESIDENTS INSPECT THE SHOP WINDOWS AT MIDNIGHT.—Drawn by P. S. Newell.

THE CHRISTMAS-TREE.

BUYING CHRISTMAS PRESENTS.—Drawn by Alice Barber Stephens.

A CHRISTMAS HYMN.—Drawn by Arthur I. Keller.

CHRISTMAS—GATHERING EVERGREENS.

CHRISTMAS OUT OF DOORS.

10

SANTA CLAUS' BEST GIFT

"THE WAITS SING UNDER MY WINDOW."

HE KNEW JUST WHAT HE WANTED

BACHELOR AT CHRISTMAS: "ER—I WANT TO GET PRESENTS FOR—ER—ABOUT SEVEN NIECES AND—ER—FIVE OR SIX NEPHEWS VARYING IN AGE FROM 'Y MONTHS TO—SAY—EIGHT YEARS."

13

SANTA CLAUS AND HIS PRESENTS.

"UNDER THE CHRISTMAS TAPERS SHINE THE OLD FACES FAIR!"

REHEARSING THE CHRISTMAS HYMNS

16

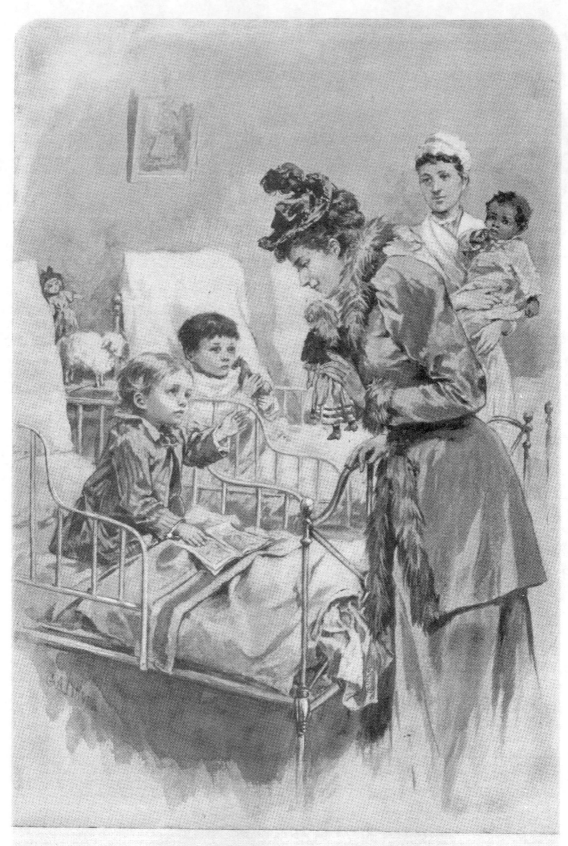

OUR CHRISTMAS VISIT TO THE CHILDREN'S HOSPITAL.
Drawn by Miss G. A. Davis.

AT THE CHILDREN'S HOSPITAL.
"My papa bought me a Shetland pony for Christmas."
"My mama gave me a little gold watch an' a blue sled."
From the next bed—"Huh! *I'se* dot a woolly lamb!"

SANTA CLAUS PAYING HIS USUAL CHRISTMAS VISIT TO HIS YOUNG FRIENDS IN THE UNITED STATES.

THE CHRISTMAS CHARIOT—THE COMING OF THE PLUM-PUDDING.

A Gilded Christmas

J. Curtis Smith

Prologue

It was 6:00 am, again. A time I have been getting up to for years. I walked to the small kitchen area of my small suburban apartment.

I really enjoy my church; the ladies in my Sunday school class are lovely women.

I drank my coffee down and ate a boiled egg from lunch yesterday. "Lord I hope it doesn't bother me and give me gas this morning in class", I thought.

I put my Sunday clothes on and was just about to head to church. As I walked out the door, I realized today was my day to tell of "My Most Memorable Christmas."

These blocks seem really long now days, but I've been walking these blocks for some sixty plus years now. The automobiles have taken the place of horse and carriage now, but the people are still just as rude.

I'm early as usual, I take the back chair and I lay my bible onto the large long heavy wooden table. I notice where people have carved their love interests in the top of the large table. Some date back to 1920, Tommy loves Sarah, Billy loves Tina, 1931.

I love coming to Sunday school early. It seems so quiet and peaceful when the large church is empty. I remember when this church held about one hundred or so people, now church service is held twice with over two hundred.

The other ladies are starting to arrive, Marie, Helen, Miss Olen, Mrs. Bergen, Mrs. Beck, and Colleta.

They all sit down. We discussed a little bit about Christmas shopping and about family coming in for the holidays.

It was quite for a minute or two and I noticed that all the ladies were staring at me.

"Taddie", "It's your turn"

"*Taddie!*"

I guess I was soaking it all in. I was day dreaming about all the Christmas's past and my family.

"*Taddie*" it's your turn to tell us ladies about your most memorable Christmas."

"Oh, I'm sorry ladies", "Sure", said Taddie.

"I hope this one won't put you girls to sleep."

I have so many great memories of Christmas but, this one is the one I cherish most.

It was 1880 . . . .

I guess my most memorable Christmas was when I was nine years old.

It was a cold time, 1880 was a cold hard year for me and my sisters.

You see, mom had been dead for six months and we had nowhere to go, but try and stay in that cold basement room.

We knew we must all stick together to survive the times.

My oldest sister, her name was Ella, just fifteen at the time, posed as our mother several times. Back then people would come and place you in state work camps until you got older. But, Ella was never gonna let that happen.

Ella and Lottie worked at the textile mill in New York City. Even though they were only 15 and 12 years old, they needed young women to slide between the looms, bring thread, oil the working looms.

The small figures and good eyes of young girls were a plus. Also it seemed that they could pay the young girls less than adults.

Ella and Lottie worked for two cents an hour. That was less than half of what they paid the adult women, but together they made just enough to pay the rent in that cold basement where we lived.

Times were different back then. The toilet us girls used was a five gallon wood can that had once held pig lard. When it got half full, we climbed up the basement stairs and would throw it out at night time. We would usually; all three walk out there, because at night it was dangerous. There was always somebody getting kidnapped or even taken advantage of. Most times, all three of us walked together, daylight or dark.

At times, the old man Mr. May, came by the basement for rent, asking for Cora our mom; Ella and Lottie would always pay him the rent and give him some excuse that Cora was busy. It seemed to pacify him or he just really didn't care, as long as the rent was paid. We usually walked to the general merchandise store on the corner and bought food. We would always try and save some money but it seemed at least one or two nights before payday we would go to sleep hungry.

Hunger, that's something I remember well. We would usually heat water and mix it with corn mill, sometimes milk if we could make it last. One meal a day!

The days of hunger seemed to get more frequent. I would stay locked in the basement room by day begging for Ella to let me go to work with her.

Then one day Ella came home and said, "Alright Taddie", "I asked Mr. Covel if you could come to work at the mill." He asked me how old you were cause; he knew how old me and Lottie were. I told him you were 11 years old. "So tomorrow you must act a little older."

"Thank you sister", "I will, I promise."

The morning whistles were blowing their wake up alarms at the mills and factories.

I could feel Ella tugging on my shoulder but it seemed way to early to get up. I could hear her preaching and then yelling, so I got up, washed at the water bowl and got my dress and stockings on.

Me, Ella, and Lottie joined the hundreds of others that morning walking to the mill. I remember asking Ella "Why was everyone carrying little buckets and little bags." She just kept saying "Nothing just walk", "I didn't know back then but, those were lunch buckets."

We arrived at the textile mill and Ella grabbed my hand and said "Come on."

We walked upstairs and it seemed like we were on top of the world. You could look down at all the women and machines. I remember the clicking and moving of all the machines was very loud.

The inside looked like it was snowing with all the little lint flakes floating in the air. I knew then why Ella and Lottie dusted off for thirty minutes every day before coming in the basement.

Bobbin Girl by Winslow Homer

Ella was lightly knocking on a big glass door where an older man was writing on a chalk board.

He turned and walked to us and Ella said "Okay act older."

The man was dressed in a brown suit, a white wrinkled shirt and a black bow tie. I remember his shoes more than anything. They looked new.

The man looked down at me and said "Ella are you sure she's eleven." "She looks more like eight maybe nine."

"Well sir" "She's always looked young, but she's a hard worker", Ella stated.

"What's your name", he asked.

"Taddie"!

"What's your name?" asked Taddie.

It's Mr. Covel, "do you really want to work here?"

"Yes Mr. Covel, me and my sister, oh, I mean my mother said it was okay and I could work for a while for some, some, new shoes."

Mr. Covel looked at me, then looked at Ella. He paused for a minute.

"Hmm, she seems awful small," he paused for a bit "Okay, she can bring the girls bobbins of thread *ONLY*, till I say different." "Same pay two cents an hour", "if she is agreeable to that, then she can start."

"Ella, show her the bobbin room and loom machines."

"Thank you so much Mr. Covel", "Thank you."

"I don't know why you thank me, just get back to work!"

So that's what I did, I took bobbins to the machines.

I did that for about two months till it was the beginning of December.

One day me and my sisters showed up and one of the workers told Ella, that Mr. Covel wanted to see her and me.

"I told you to act older", is all Ella kept saying.

Ella knocked on the door of Mr. Covel's office and this time he yelled "come on in"; so we opened the door and walked on in.

"Did you want to see me", asked Ella.

"Yes, please sit down" Ella.

"My daughter is back from boarding school and I was wondering, well, if Taddie could stay up here and play with her till after the first, that's when she goes back to Boarding school."

"I mean if, if that's okay with your mother."

"Sure", Ella stated

"I will have to ask mom that is."

"Also" stated Mr. Covel, "I will pay you, Taddie, an Lottie, and extra one cent an hour. Not especially for this, but you three are dependable, hard, working girls."

"Thank you very much Mr. Covel", "Thank you", said Taddie.

"Well, you two girls, let me know in the morning",

"Yes we will."

The girls walked down stairs, with a good feeling about them.

Ella was immediately thinking of the extra two dollars and sixteen cents a week.

She was thinking about heavier coats for the winter, new stockings and of course a little more food at the house.

That afternoon the three girls dusted and picked the lint off of each other, with smiles.

Ella then stated "After supper we need a family meeting."

Lottie washed her hands and her face then she grabbed a medium size bowl off the shelf. It was last night's supper, a handful of beans and corn meal mash.

Taddie looked at Lottie putting it back on the pot belly stove and grumbled "Not again", we've had that all week.

"Well Taddie after our next pay, I will see if I can buy a little better variety," stated Ella.

Supper was over, faster than ever and after Ella washed all the bowls and the spoons, she announced that we must all set down and discuss our future earnings.

She announced with the good news of pay raises and the added benefit of Taddie working, now we should finally get a little ahead. We were making eleven dollars and fifty two cents a month, now we have jumped to twenty five dollars and ninety two cents, more than double.

"The rent is five dollars a month, coal for the stove has been around a dollar fifty, and bare minimum food was three sometimes five."

"I think let's stay the same for a couple of months and save some money for some new shoes or stockings, what do ya think?"

Lottie spoke up and said "You're the oldest Ella, whatever you think."

"Taddie?"

" I think we should buy more food, Now"!

"Okay", "I will try and buy just a little more food, while we save and see how it all goes", stated Ella.

That night, the girl's all thought about the rich's that were to come.

But also, that night, deep in their sleep, visitors came to the basement house.

The noise was unbearable, squealing, yelling and slapping.

The visitors were hungry and mean, some were as big as cats, but all seemed really aggressive.

Taddie was bit several times by at least two different rats and Lottie and Ella beat them off with their hands and feet.

The night was a long night, for the massive rats decided to stay until close to daylight.

There was no water to clean up with and Taddie was bleeding from two bites on her legs.

Ella stepped outside and it was lightly snowing she walked upstairs to Ruby Finns and asked for a pitcher of water and a cloth to clean with.

Ruby obliged, but was headed out the door. Ruby asked "is your water spicket broke again Ella?" "No Ruby, we had giant rats coming out of the hole where the pipe comes out of the wall, and I'm not about to try it right now!"

Oh no, not again, it seems like every time it starts to get cold they come in. Take what you need."

"Thank you Ruby", said Ella.

Ella took the pitcher back to the basement and the girls washed off. This time Ella and Lottie, cleaned Taddie up put her good clothes on her. Today, Taddie was going to spend with Annibel Covel.

"It's snowing outside Taddie." "So I want you to wear Lottie's sweater, I can't let you go out without some kind of protection."

"Where is yours and Lotties sweater", Taddie asked.

"We will be fine" Ella said.

We walked out of the basement and the light snow had turned to a much heavier snow. It was swirling around landing in our hair and into our eyes. Locked in each other hands we finally made it to the mill.

Mr. Covel was standing at the rail, looking down as if he had lost a quarter dollar.

You could see the relief on his face when we walked into the mill.

Ella walked Taddie up the stairs.

"You are late", "Ella you know I must suspend an hour of pay and put it on file", said Mr. Covel.

"Hi Taddie", "come with me and I will introduce you to Annibel", said Mr. Covel.

Mr. Covel opened his door and Annibel was sitting very politely on the small leather sofa that was against the wall. She was wearing a very clean, ironed white dress, a light blue apron, with light blue stockings. Her shoes were shiny black with a strap and a shiny brass buckle on the side. Annibel was a pretty girl with blue eyes and brown hair.

"Annibel this is Taddie Fandren", "her sisters work here. I have to go down stairs. You two have fun". I walked over to Annibel and stuck my hand out and said, "I'm Taddie." She looked at me and said;

"Do you see my father?"

Taddie looked, "No, he went down stairs."

"I have to be a lady around my father and mother. That's what they keep telling me. I'm Annibel", as she stuck her hand out and shook.

"My father, Mr. Covel, and my mother, Mrs. Covel have spent a great deal of money for me to be a lady. They send me to school at Valenta's Finishing School in upstate New York. So, where do you go to school at?"

Taddie looked at her and said, "First off", "I don't know who my father is, I have never met him. My mother died about a year ago. She died from some coughing disease."

"My sisters have taught me to read some, but I really don't know what a school is."

"That's alright", Annibel stated.

"It's a lot of fancy girls, learning to talk proper, and eat proper."

"The teachers are stern and not very fun either."

"What do you do that's fun Taddie?"

I remember looking at her and was thinking.

"Before mom died she made me a dollie out of a coffee sack. We use to pretend that.., that…, never mind."

"*That, what?*" asked Annibel.

"That we were rich, that we lived in a big house and had servants. We would pretend to put fancy clothes on it; but it was just pretend."

"Oh", said Annibel.

"Let's just talk", said Annibel.

"I will tell you stories I have read about at school and then if you have any you can tell me". Annibel told story after story. The working day flew by and the whistle blew ending the shift.

30

Annibel asked Taddie if she was going to be back tomorrow, she said "sure."

Just before she walked out the door Annibel yelled out *"hold it."*

"You must have cut yourself, you leg is bleeding through your stocking!"

"Oh, no, it's bites!" "We had a pack of rats come through our room last night. I will be fine."

Annibel looked at Taddie with a sad face and didn't say another word.

That afternoon after the normal corn mash supper, the girls stuffed small boards and strips of potatoe sacks into the three inch hole where the lead pipe came into the basement.

"Tomorrow we will need to go to the railroad dock and collect more wood and maybe find some coal for our stove too, okay Lottie."

"Sure Ella, before we go, can we swing by the church and see if they have a coat for each of us?", asked Lottie.

"Lottie, you know they never have any, but we can look." "Taddie?" "How did your stay with Annibel go?" Taddie just started talking about all the stories that Annibel was telling her.

The morning whistles blowing and all the girls were tucked under the heavy blankets. They had fallen asleep listening to the stories that Taddie had been telling them.

They got dressed and couldn't wait for Taddie to learn more stories.

Everyday Taddie would come back with more stories, even the stories of her and Annibel playing with some of the Fancy porcelain dolls Annibel had brought to the mill. They wanted to know what it felt like to hold a doll and what the dolls were wearing. Even what Annibel had named them.

It was about four days from Christmas day. Taddie walked into the room and Annibel was excited.

"Taddie, my father and mother just bought me this new book! ***"A Visit From St Nicholas"***, "Who is Saint Nicholas", Taddie asked.

"*What*, have you not heard of Santa Claus?"

He has brought me most of my dollies!

"No, why did he bring'em to you, does he work at the store?"

"No, No, silly"

"Let me recite it to you", stated Annibel

"It was written by a father that personally seen Santa Claus." "His name is Clement C. Moore. He was drawn by a man that seen Santa Claus many times too; his name is Thomas Nast."

A Visit From
St. Nicholas.

By Clement C. Moore.

Twas the Night before Christmas, when all through the house
Not a creature was stirring, not even a mouse;
The stockings were hung by the chimney with care,
In the hopes that St. Nicholas soon would be there;
The children were nestled all snug in their beds,
While visions of sugar-plums danced in their heads;
And mama in her kerchief and I in my cap,
Had just settled down for a long winter's nap –
When out on the lawn there arose such a clatter,
I sprang from the bed to see what was the matter;
Away to the window I flew like a flash,
Tore open the shutters and threw up the sash,
The moon, on the breast of the new-fallen snow,
Gave a lustre of mid-day to objects below.
When, what to my wondering eyes should appear,
But a miniature sleigh and eight tiny rein-deer,
With a little old driver, so lively and quick,
I knew in a moment it must be St. Nick.
More rapid than eagles his coursers they came,
And he whistled, and shouted and called them by name;
"Now, Dasher! now, Dancer! now, Prancer! Now, Vixen!
On! Comet, on! Cupid, on! Donder and Blitzen-
To the top of the porch! to the top of the wall!
Now, dash away, dash way, dash away, all!"
As leaves that before the wild hurricane fly,
When they meet with an obstacle, mount to the sky,
So, up to the house-top the coursers they flew,
With sleigh full of toys – and St. Nicholas too.

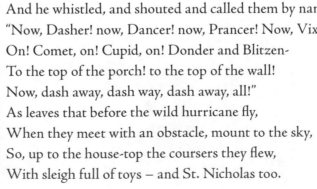

And then in a twinkling I heard on the roof
The prancing and pawing of each little hoof.
As I drew in my head, and was turning around,
Down the chimney St. Nicholas came with bound.
He was dressed all in fur, from his head to his foot,
And his clothes were all tarnish'd with ashes and soot;
A bundle of toys he had flung on his back,
And he look'd like a pedlar just opening his pack.
His eyes-how they twinkled! his dimples, how merry!
His cheeks were like roses, his nose like a cherry;
His droll little mouth was drawn up like a bow,
And the beard on his chin was as white as the snow.
The stump of a pipe he held tight in his teeth,
And the smoke, it encircled his head like a wreath.
He had a broad face and a little round belly
That shook, when he laugh'd, like a bowl full of jelly.
He was chubby and plump ; a right jolly old elf;
And I laughed when I saw him, in spite of myself.
A wink of his eye, and a twist of his head,
Soon gave me to know I had nothing to dread.
He spoke not a word, but went straight to his work,
And filled all the stockings; then turned with a jirk,
And laying his finger aside of his nose,
And giving a nod, up the chimney he rose.
He sprang to his sleigh, to his team gave a whistle,
And away they all flew like the down of a thistle;
But I heard him exclaim ere he drove out of sight,
"Happy Christmas to all, and to all a good night!"

"Read it again Annibel", "please!"

We read it for hours I even memorized it. We looked at the pictures in it, and Annibel told me stories of how the Christmas tree fully decorated and stockings and presents were all beside it. She painted a beautiful picture in my mind.

Before we knew it the whistles were blowing. I started out the door and Annibel looked at me and said *"Wait"*, *"Wait* here take this book, I have read it enough." "Besides I'll have my father buy me a new one."

"Are you sure, I don't want to get in trouble", said Taddie.

"I'm sure, Nothing will happen."

So Taddie took the book, and walked down the stairs.

While on the floor with the cleaning crew, Mr. Covel seen Taddie walking out the door with the new book.

That afternoon the dinner bell was ringing and Annibel came running down the stairs of the big beautiful house; stopping every so often to slide down the fancy, shiny, handrails.

Mr. Covel was walking out of the study room with a pipe in his mouth, setting it into an ash tray that was at the door's entrance. Mrs. Covel, was gracefully walking to the dinner room.

The dinner room was usually the only room and time that the Covel's got to see each other.

The big dining table could sit fourteen people, but there usually just the three of them, unless there was a party.

Annibel was already asking what Santa may bring her, and that she had been nice.

That's when Silas Covel opened up and said "Annibel?" "I noticed that Taddie walked out of the mill with your new book today!" "Did she take it or did she just borrow it?"

"Father, I gave the book to her." "She didn't know who Santa Claus, or Saint Nicholas are." "I told her that if she believes and is good that he will visit her too." "That's right isn't it father?"

Mr. Covel looked at his young innocent daughter, for several seconds.

"She has never even seen a Christmas tree either father." "It sadden me too", stated Annibel.

"Well, you know Annibel that if they don't truly believe, then St. Nicholas won't visit." "Plus there are some people who are naughty and some people move from place to place."

"I know father, but it seems like Taddie was so happy to even know about Santa, and to see all the pictures in the book!" "She said she will be quick to bed Christmas Eve." "I hope Santa visits her and her sisters."

After supper Mrs. Covel asked Silas what he was gonna do about the Fondren girls.

"I don't know, maybe Santa can find them?"

The week flew by, it was a cheerful day.

Taddie spent the whole day delivering bobbins because Annibel stayed at home.

I can remember everybody talking about preparing turkey's, ducks, and even Christmas pudding.

The work day flew by. The whistle was blowing, and the cleaning crew was the only people left. Mr. Covel was closing the plant down. The only day of the year the plant was down.

It was around eight o'clock Christmas Eve and the machines were all quite.

Mr. Covel locked the door as he had done only twenty times before.

The door of the basement was pounding that afternoon and it was the church ladies. They handed out bibles and two cotton bags labeled flour. Inside were walnuts, pecans, peanuts and little cardboard cut outs of Jesus on the cross. We always looked forward to this.

"Alright Lottie and Taddie, we can either eat this today or wait till Christmas day while we are looking for wood and coal", stated Ella.

"Well Ella, Santa will be here tomorrow", stated Taddie.

"Taddie, if he doesn't show up don't be disappointed; just remember the reason we celebrate Christmas is the birth of our Savior, Jesus Christ."

"I know Ella, but I sent him a letter that Annibel helped me write, she said she would even send it."

"Well just remember."

Taddie ate all her nuts, even the orange that was in her bag. Ella yelled at her to save the bag for we can possibly make a pair of light gloves out of them.

The girls were all nestled in their bed.

It was so quite in the basement, "I hope there won't be any rats stirring tonight." Were Taddie's last words before she fell asleep.

When Taddie and Lottie fell asleep, Ella got up snuck into a wooden chest that held all her private things. Inside her chest Ella pulled out a tree branch; she had tried to find a branch with lots of limbs on it. Maybe this can work for a Christmas tree, Ella thought.

Ella had collected the threads and lint for several weeks to put onto the branch to decorate it similar to the ones in the big new Woolworths window.

Ella then placed a small candle in front; which she would use to make it glow when her sister awoke. Ella also took some resin from the mill and attached the branch to a base, she had made from an end of thread bobbin she took from work. It was in the discard bin, so she knew it was not to be used again.

Ella then pulled two pair of long stockings from her wooden chest; she had them wrapped in wax paper. Just as she set them down on a table, by the homemade Christmas tree; A knock on the door. Then another knock just a little louder.

It was way late, Ella thought. She waited for a minute, but they still kept knocking. Finally she heard a voice, it sounded familiar but still she was nervous.

Ella, grabbed a skillet, then slowly opened the door.

It was hard for her to see because it was snowing and all she could see was a dark figure with the background of a gas powered street lamp.

"Ella, this is Santa Claus, you know Saint Nicholas. I finally found your house after all these years."

The dark figure entered the basement and all Ella could see was Red with some white furry linings. Ella couldn't see his face for the red hood, but the man brought a tree, *a real Christmas tree*. He then placed three white angels on it.

Santa then opened a bag, pulled out 3 boxes. They were all wrapped in beautiful wrapping with fancy ribbons and bows. He laid them beside the tree. "I noticed no stockings laid out", so he opened up and pulled out three pairs of stockings. He then pulled three heavy wool coats from the bag.

He didn't say much except about the stockings. How he guessed the lengths. Then Ole Saint Nick, looked back and said Merry Christmas to all, and goodnight.

The red shadowy figure then left the basement. The next morning Ella told us the story that happened.

We played with the dollies all morning. We admired the stockings and our new heavy coats also.

While we were cleaning up and putting the fancy wrappings and bows in our personal boxes, I noticed an envelope.

"Ella, there is an envelope by the tree." Ella bent down and looked, it read "From Santa" Ella opened up the envelope and it read

> *Dear Ella, Lottie, Taddie*
> *I'm sorry I have passed your house for so many years.*
> *I hope you, always believe and have faith.*
> *Santa*

"The letter to all of us seemed amazing, but also the two five dollar bills, helped us get on our feet."

"That Christmas we ate good and told everyone about Saint Nicholas."

"That Christmas started something good in our lives. It lasted till the Textile mill closed down. Santa stopped visiting. I was sixteen at the time, and Ella had married. Lottie and I lived with Ella and Samuel for just a while before we were married off. But we always celebrate Christmas with our families with the birth of Jesus Christ and **a visit from Saint Nicholas.**"

"Oh, one last things ladies."

"The Christmas book that Annibel had given us that Christmas; Its edges are frayed and worn, the pictures that were lively and full of vibrant colors are dimmer now, but every Christmas I put it out on my coffee table, and thumb through it ever so slowly. I still think about the joy and fun and all the excitement we enjoyed, with the thought of Santa Claus coming to visit."

"It warms my heart at least one time a year to know that he still visits my house." I told the ladies.

The faces on all the women in the class were somber, but yet happy. It seemed that their Christmas stories didn't quite match up to Taddies. It was evident because they stayed in class all the way through the morning church services listening to Taddie's story.

Taddie picked up her bible off the hard wood table from whence the older ladies were all gathered and walked to the door. She looked at the big clock just above the entry way twelve thirty five; she then walked into the big empty church hall. She stood for a minute to look back at the big wooden cross and walked on through. She giggled for a minute and quietly said, "Not a creature is stirring, not even a mouse", and walked on home.

COLLIER'S

CHRISTMAS NUMBER

MDCCCXCVIII   PRICE 25 CENTS

"THE CHRIST FROM HIS CROSS HAS VANISHED, AND A LITTLE
CHILD STANDS THERE."

"JE VOUS SALUE, MARIE" (HAIL, MARY).

FROM THE PAINTING BY LUC OLIVIER MERSON. PURCHASED BY THE EXPOSITION FUND FOR THE ATLANTA, GEORGIA, MUSEUM OF FINE ARTS.

NUNS DRESSING UP THE "CRIB" FOR CHRISTMAS IN THE CHAPEL OF A CONVENT.

40

"CLEAR AND SWEET THE NUNS ARE SINGING."

THE EARTH.

CHRISTMAS FAIRIES.

Drawn by F. A. Carter

"IS 'OO SANTY-CLAUS?"

Painted by Louis Loeb

CHRISTMAS IN THE SOUTH—BEFORE THE WAR

 WHEN Christmas times dey comes along,
    It's den I takes my stan':
My voice I lif' fer Christmas gif'
    Fum my ole Marster's han'.
'En my ole Miss—she come along
En hear me sing dat Christmas song:
      My voice I lif'
      Fer Christmas gif'—
Oh, don't you do me wrong!

De darkies fum de cabins come
    En lif' dey hat—like dis!
"Christmas gif', ole Marster—
    Christmas gif', ole Miss!"
En den I gits my dram, en den
I dances with de yuther men:
      My voice I lif'
      Fer Christmas gif'—
I'se happy once agen!

                    FRANK L. STANTON.

CHRISTMAS IN VIRGINIA—A PRESENT FROM THE GREAT HOUSE.—[Drawn by W. L. Sheppard.]

A NEW SUIT FOR CHRISTMAS.—From a Photograph by the Berlin Photograph Company.—See Page 296.

"WHO DONE SAY DAT DEY AIN'T NO SANDY CLAWS?"

DRAWN BY E. W. KEMBLE

WIDE AWAKE—CHRISTMAS-EVE.—[Drawn by Sol. Eytinge, Jun.]

49

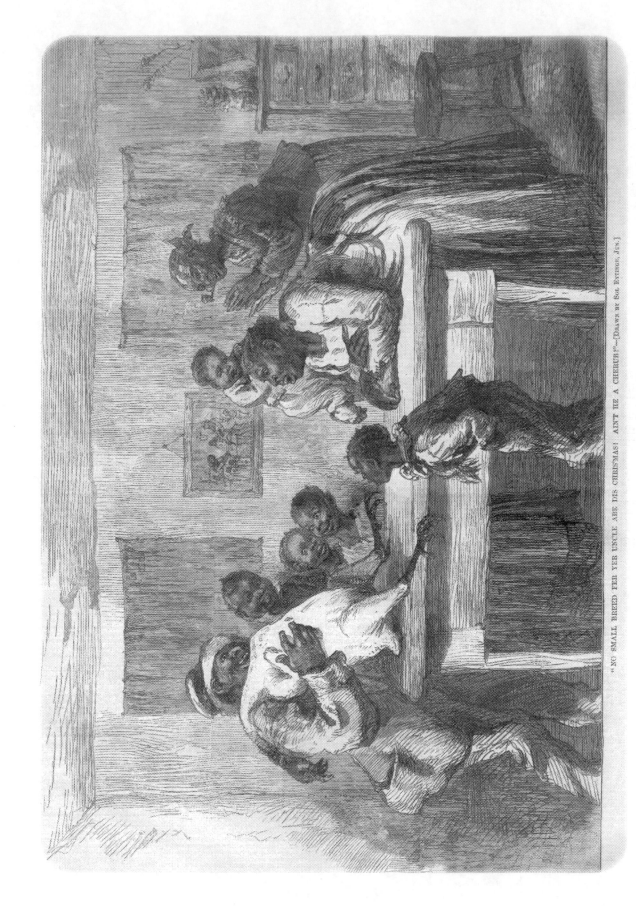

"NO SMALL BREED YER UNCLE ABE HIS CHRIS'MAS! AIN'T HE A CHERUB?"—[Drawn by Sol. Eytinge, Jun.]

IN OLD VIRGINIA.—"DE CHRISTMAS DINNER AM SAFE FU' SHO'."—DRAWN BY GILBERT GAUL.

AN ASSISTED EMIGRANT.—Drawn by Charles Broughton.—[See Page 1194.]

FAITH—WAITING FOR SANTA CLAUS.—[From a Water-color Drawing by M. Woolf.]

LIGHT IN THE WINDOW.—[See Poem on Page 6.]

A CHRISTMAS PIE.

THE LAST GUEST—THE MORNING AFTER CHRISTMAS

CHRISTMAS MARKETING—THE VEGETARIAN.

ement to Collier's Weekly
Christmas 1898

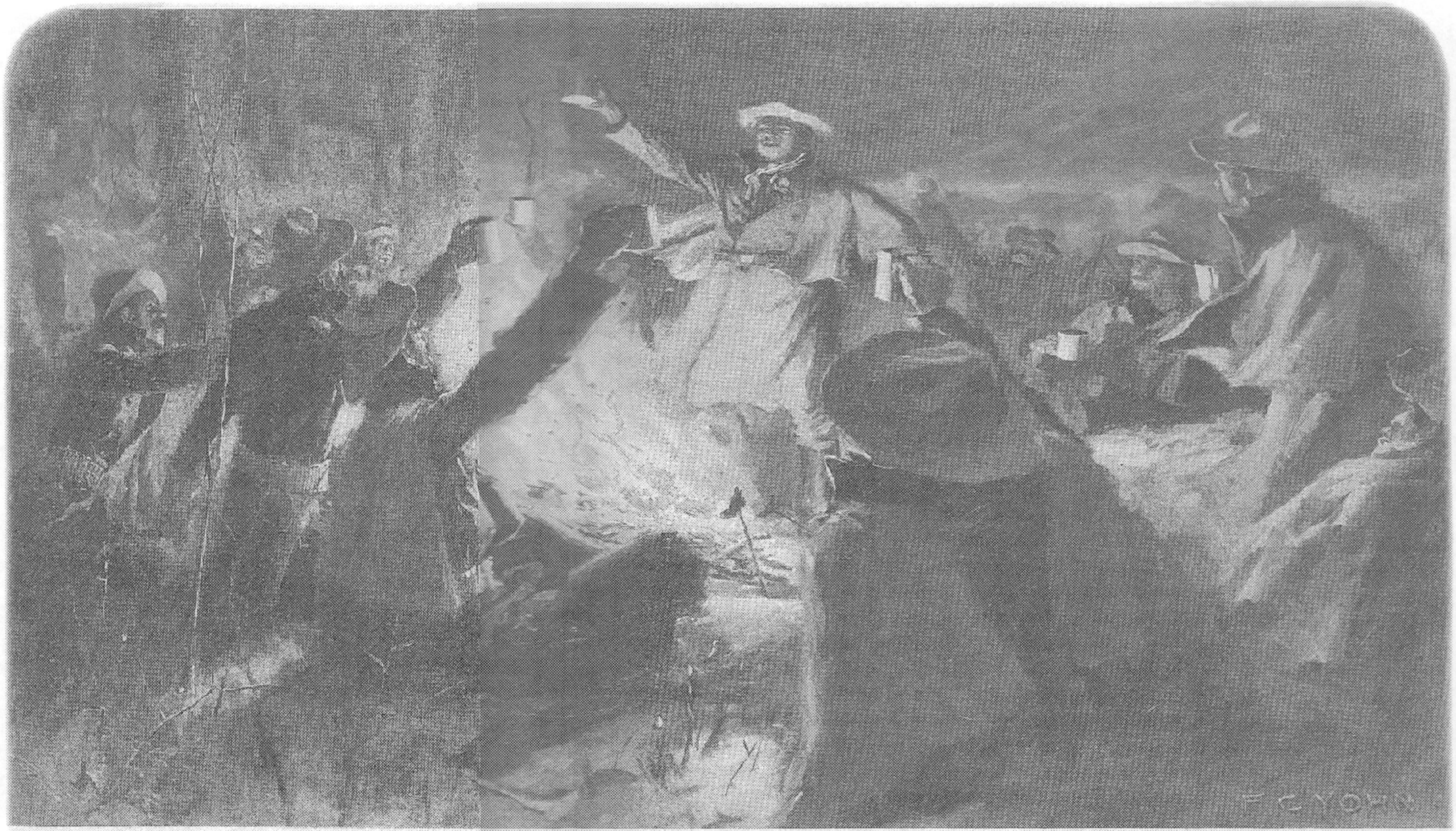

"THE TROOPER'S TOAST"

UNITED STATES REGULAR CAVALRYMEN IN PURSUIT OF RESERVATION INDIANS ARE OVERTAKEN BY A BLINDING SNOWSTORM IN THE FOOTHILLS ON CHRISTMAS EVE. THEY PICKET OUT THEIR HORSES, GATHER ROUND THE CAMP-FIRE AND DRINK A TOAST IN "SNOW-WATER GROG" TO HOME AND THE LOVED ONES FAR AWAY

PAINTED BY F. C. YOHN

drawn by H. Reuterdahl

THOUGHTS OF HOME
CHRISTMAS EVE WITH THE FLEET IN MANILA BAY 1898

THE FINDING OF CHRISTMAS.—"*He sank down under a pine-tree where the snow had drifted away.*"—[See story on preceding pages.]

THE CONVICT'S CHRISTMAS—A LETTER FROM HOME.

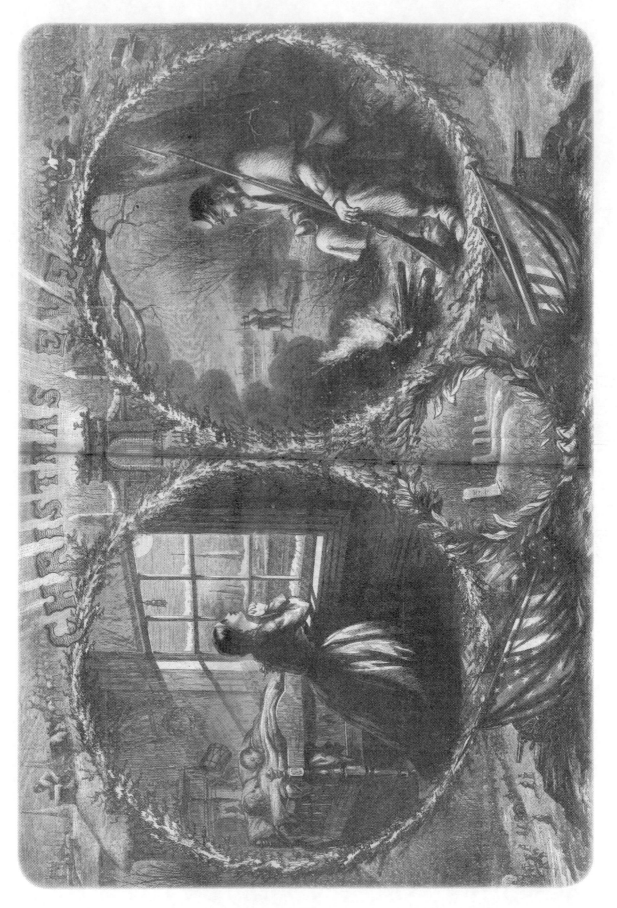

SANTA CLAUS IN CAMP.—[See Page 6.]

CHRISTMAS EVE

64

"HELLO, SANTA CLAUS!"

65

CHRISTMAS POST.

67

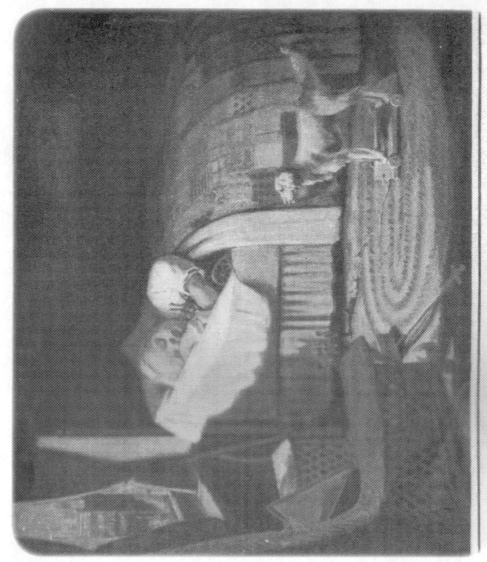

THE CHRISTMAS DREAM.—Drawn by Jules Taverner.—(See Page 1226.)

THE AWAKENING OF SANTA CLAUS

IN THE WRONG ROOM.—SANTA-CLAUS: "WHAT A BLUNDERING OLD GOOSE I AM! She doesn't want toys and dolls and cake."

71

SEEING SANTA CLAUS,

HELLO! what's the matter? Who's this that I see?
Two forms on the roof! Who on earth can they be?
It is time that the young ones were tucked in their beds,
With visions of Christmas afloat in their heads.

Now bother these boys! What the mischief, I say,
Has brought them up here, just to be in my way?
But stop! a thought strikes me. Aha! now I see:
They are waiting, the rogues, for a good look at me.

They are getting too old; they're beginning to doubt;
They think there is something they'd like to find out.
The very same passion that wrecked Mother Eve
Has entered the souls of these boys, I believe;

And thirsting for knowledge, they're here on the roof;
The stories about me they'll put to the proof.
Young children I love, with their sweet cunning ways,
But who doesn't hate boys in their roundabout days?

Oh dear, how they stare! What on earth shall I do?
Do you think, you young scamps, I'll be conquered by you?
You seem very bright, with your wide-open eyes,
And you'd think it so smart to take me by surprise.

It's a very fine plan, my young rascals, but pause
Ere you get up a trap to catch old Santa Claus.
And then, I'm afraid, if I let you succeed—
Oh, it never would do; you'd regret it, indeed.

'Tis a wonderful vision you see in your dreams:
Like a king in his glory old Santa Claus seems;
With a coat of white ermine as pure as the snow,
You think me a gorgeous old gray-beard, I know.

You fancy my eyes are as bright as your own;
That I dwell in a palace, and sit on a throne;
That I own a vast kingdom 'way up in the North,
And only the night before Christmas come forth;

That I've nothing to do but to pack up my toys,
And call once a year on the girls and the boys;
That my reindeers are harnessed and ready to fly
Quick, quick o'er the roofs and the chimneys so high.

Ah, what would you say could you know the sad truth,
Long ago in your service I wore out my youth,
Just think of the burdens I've borne on my back,
And the terrible weight of old Santa Claus' pack!

The sprite that you love is all blackened with soot;
Poor Santa Claus' coat is as black as your boot;
In a shriveled-up elf, with a phiz old and grim,
And a hump on his back, would you recognize him?

It is better, my boys, that you never should know
How far from the truth your bright fancies go.
It's all for your good. In the shadow I'll stay
Up here on the chimney till you go away.

CAUGHT!

THE WATCH ON CHRISTMAS EVE.—[DRAWN BY C. S. REINHART.]

EARLY BIRDS; OR, CHRISTMAS MORNING.—[FROM THE PAINTING BY J. O. EATON, OWNED BY E. W. CLARK, PHILADELPHIA.]

MERRY CHRISTMAS.

(See Poem, Page 1260.)

SANTA CLAUS'S RETURN HOME.

DRAWN BY W. A. ROGERS.

The WONDERS of SANTA CLAUS.

CHAPTER I.

CONCERNING SANT. "CLAUS.—HIS ASTONISHING CRADLE.—HIS BEAUTIFUL GIFTS FOR ALL GOOD CHILDREN.—AND HIS REAL NAME.

BEYOND the ocean many a mile,
And many a year ago,
There lived a wonderful queer old man
In a wonderful house of snow;
And every little boy and girl,
As Christmas Eves arrive,
No doubt will be very glad to hear,
The old man is still alive.

In his house upon the top of a hill,
And almost out of sight,
He keeps a great many elves at work,
All working with all their might,
To make a million of pretty things,
Cakes, sugar-plums, and toys,
To fill the stockings, hung up you know
By the little girls and boys.

It would be a capital treat be sure,
A glimpse of his wondrous shop;
But the queer old man when a stranger comes,
Orders every elf to stop;
And the house, and work, and workmen all
Instantly take a twist,
And just you may think you are there,
They are off in a frosty mist.

But upon a time a cunning boy
Saw this sign upon the gate,
Nobody can ever enter here
Who lies a-bed too late;
Let all who expect a good stocking full,
Not spend too much time in play;
Keep book and work all the while in mind,
And be up by the peep of day.

A holiday morning would scarce suffice
To tell what was making there;
Wagons and dolls, whistles and birds,
And elephants most rare;
Wild monkeys drest like little men,
And dogs that could almost bark,
Watches, that, if they only had wheels,
Might beat the old clock in the Park.

Whole armies of little soldier folk,
All marching in grand review,
And turning up their eyes at the girls,
As the City soldiers do;
Engines, fast hurrying to a fire,
And many a little fool
A-trudging after them through the streets,
Instead of going to school.

Tin fiddles, and trumpets made of wood,
That will play as good a tune
As a Scotch bag-piper could perform
From Christmas-day till June;
Horses, with riders upon their backs,
Coaches, and carts, and gigs,
Each trying its best to win the race,
Like the Democrats and Whigs.

Some little fellows turning a crank,
And others beating a drum;
Little pianos, so! canst
You could almost hear them thrum.
Tea-sets and tables quite complete,
With ladies sitting around,
Chatting as older ladies do,
But a little more profound.

Steamboats made to sail in a tub,
And fishing-smacks ahoy,
And boats and skiffs with oars and sails,
A fleet for a sailor boy;
Ships of the line, equipt for sea,
With officers and crew,
Each with a red cap on his head,
And a jacket painted blue.

Bold pewter men with pistols armed,
Like duelists so spare,
Each very wickedly taking aim,
At his little comrade's heart;
And nimble Jacks with supple joints,
That when you pull a string,
Will give you an easy lesson how
To dance the Pigeon Wing.

Ugly old women in a box,
As some younger ones ought to be,
Which, when the cover is lifted off,
Fly out most spitefully;
Ripe wooden pears like real fruit,
Somehow made to unscrew;
Kittens with mice sewed to their mouths,
And tabby cats crying mew.

Gay humming-tops that spin about,
And make a senseless sound,
Like windy representatives
In Congress often found.
Fine marbles, and rich China-men,
That you can play from taw,
As lawyers play rich clients down
The ring-pits of the law.

Bright caskets filled with jewelry,
Chains, bracelets, pins, and pearls,
All glittering with tinsel, like
Some fashionable girls;
Delightful little picture books,
And tales of Mother Goose,
More witty than most novels are;
And twenty times their use.

But it were an endless task to tell,
The length that the list extends,
Of the curious gifts the queer old man
Prepares for his Christmas friends.
Belike you are guessing who he is,
And the country whence he came.
Why, he was born in Germany,
And St. Nicholas is his name.

In London he gave them rounds of beef,
And two plum-puddings a-piece,
Then stepped to Windsor palace of course,
To see his royal niece.
He gave her a little Parliament,
Discussing a knotty bill,
And two or three nuts for them to crack,
And a birch to keep them still.

And now, said he, for St. Petersburg!
Over the cold North Sea,
And up the Baltic he sped in haste,
And was there when the clock struck three.
He hied to the palace of the Czar,
And clambered in at the dome;
A great many stockings were hung around,
But the folks were not at home.

He gave them little Siberian mines,
With little men in chains,
Who strove to avenge their country's wrongs,
And were sent there for their pains.
He left the Emperor a map,
With Russia cut in four,
As much as to say, great Muscovite,
Your sway may soon be o'er.

CHAPTER II.

HOW ST. NICHOLAS GOT ALL HIS PACKAGES READY, IN ORDER TO START AT SUNDOWN, UPON HIS LONG JOURNEY. HOW HE WENT TO AMSTERDAM, PARIS, DUBLIN, LONDON, AND ST. PETERSBURG.

December's four and twentieth day
Through its course was almost run,
St. Nicholas stood at his castle door
Awaiting the setting sun.
His goods were packed in a great balloon,
Near by were his horse and sleigh;
He had his skates upon his feet,
And a ship getting under weigh.

For he was to travel by sea and land,
And sometimes through the air,
And then to skim on the rivers smooth,
When the ice his weight would bear.
The wind blew keen, and the snow fell fast,
But not a whit cared he;
For he knew a myriad little hearts
Were longing that night to see.

Away he flew to Amsterdam,
As soon as the sun went down,
And left whole bushels of play-things there,
For every child in town.
Then he tried his skates on the Zuyder Zee,
Southwest to Dever's Strait,
Then Southward with his horse and sleigh,
He was soon at Paris' gate.

He scaled the walls of the Tuileries,
The children were all retired,
And every stocking was hanging up,
As St. Nicholas desired.
In one he put a sceptre and crown,
In another a guillotine,
And a little man without a head,
Who King of the French had been.

He paused a while at Notre Dame,
To see the Christmas show;
Then with his grand Montgolfier
Majestically rose,
And from his splendid parachute,
A shower of bonbons threw,
For all the little ones in France,
And bade them all adieu.

Then down he drove on the River Seine,
And on the Biscay bay,
Took ship for famous Dublin town,
And London on his way.
In Dublin what do you think he left,
For the hearty Irish boys?
Why, bags of potatoes instead of cakes,
And shillalaghs instead of toys.

Then down he hastened for Italy,
To call at the Vatican,
Forgetting, until he had arrived,
The Pope is a bachelor man.
But he looked in at St. Peter's church,
And saw the whole town at prayer,
So he left a basket full at the door,
For all the good children there.

Upon the Mediterranean Sea,
He boarded his ship again,
And hoisted sail, and steered west,
To see the Queen of Spain,
And give her a legion of wooden men,
Equipt from foot to nose,
And a troop of leaden horsemen too,
The rebels to oppose.

Now all good little boys and girls
Shall have a noble treat,
Delighted presents, that will make
The holidays complete.

Upon the spire of old St. Paul's
Policeman saw him stand,
Reading his list of ancient friends,
With his leather bags in hand.
'Tis said he dropt a frozen tear,
As he looked on the streets below,
And saw what a mighty change has come
Since Christmas times ago!

Those brave old times when great mince pies
Were piled on every shelf,
And every Knickerbocker boy
Might go and help himself.
When Broadway was a path for cows,
And all the streets were lanes,
And the houses were so snug and quaint,
With their bull's-eye window-panes;

And low old-fashioned door-ways, where,
The upper part swung in,
The Dutchman could his elbows lean,
And smoke his pipe and grin.
Then doughnuts were all good to eat,
And made as big as bricks,
And 'twas not thought unmannerly
To eat as many as six.

Good simple times, when lad and lass,
In happy groups were seen,
With sled and skate for winter sports,
Around the Bowling Green,
When maidens plied the spinning-wheel,
And idlers were unknown,
And all the up-town people lived
Below the one-mile stone.

When all were good and went to church,
And heeded what they heard,
And children never learned to speak
A bad or saucy word.
With plenty smiling every where,
Like Christmas every day,
Content and love at every hearth,
O what rare times were they!

But long before all this was said,
The stockings were all filled,
And Santa-claus was skating home,
With his nose a little chilled.
He whistled as he skimmed along,
Till the day began to dawn,
Then giving a twirl in the frosty air,
St. Nicholas was gone!

CHAPTER III.

ST. NICHOLAS HURRYING AWAY FROM SPAIN, AND SETS SAIL FOR AMERICA.

O'er the Cantabrian mountains wild,
He hurried to the strand,
To meet his treasure-laden ship,
There waiting his command.
He scattered beautiful gifts around,
As he went flying past,
Then put his trumpet to his lips,
And blew a rousing blast.

Up, up my gallant sailors all,
Swiftly your anchor weigh,
The wind is fair, and we must sail,
For far America.
By wind and steam for New Amsterdam,
Three thousand miles an hour,
Onward he drove his cabin ship,
With a thousand-fairy power.

Down at the Battery he moored,
And gave a grand salute,
You cannot ....
And powder made to suit.
Then he hoisted out a score of bales,
Of his cakes, and nuts, and wares;
You would have been amazed to see
The heaps on the ferry stairs.

All's well, all's well! loud voices cried,
St. Nicholas is here!
How charming many a stocking full
In the morning will appear.

79

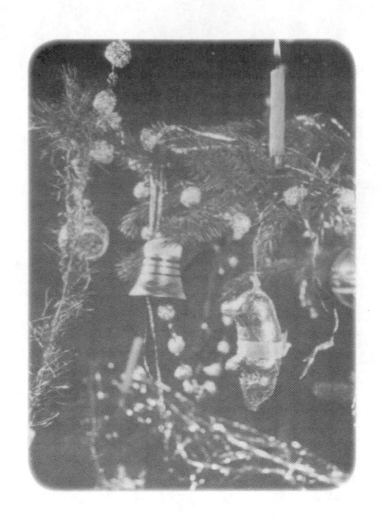

1202

87

Sheila Kinsey

Award-winning artist, Sheila Kinsey, has loved art since she was a child. In grade school, she won a Santa drawing contest and it has been a love affair with Santa ever since. Besides Santa, this Dallas artist specializes in portraits, pet portraits, still life and landscapes. Her work is primarily oil on canvas. A commissioned artist, her paintings and prints are in many homes across America. She has conducted private and group art lessons for both adults and children. Please google Sheila Kinsey fine artist to view her work.

Illustration Credits

With the exception of cropping images where needed no other changes have been made to the photographs in this book. The caliber and clarity of many photographs are limited to the technology of the day and the ability of the illustrator at the time they were made. The illustrations in this book are very old from sources that are very old, original newspapers and magazines.

Illustration Acknowledgement:

Christmas dinner behind the scenes	1901	Harpers Weekly
Christmas Waits	1901	Lawrence
Christmas season in the shopping district	1895	PS Newell
The Christmas Tree	1858	Winslow Homer
Buying Christmas Presents	1895	Alice Barber Stevens
A Christmas Hymn	1897	A.J. Keller
Christmas gathering Evergreens	1858	Winslow Homer
Christmas Outdoors	1858	Winslow Homer
Santa Claus best gift	1901	A.J. Keller
The weights sing under my window	1880	Frank Leslie Illustrated
He know just what he wanted	1910	Angus McDonall
Santa Claus in his presents	1858	Winslow Homer
Under Christmas Tapers	1880	Frank Leslie Illustrated
Rehearsing the Christmas Hymns	1901	H. W.
Singing In The Chior	1892	B. West Clinedinst
Our Christmas visit to Children Hospital	1898	G. A. Davis

At the Children Hospital	1892	J. A. Waller
Winslow Homer Santa	1858	Winslow Homer
The Christmas Chariot	1876	S. E. Waller
A Gilded Christmas	2012	J. Curtis Smith
(Bobbin Girl)	1860	Winslow Homer
(A Visit from Saint Nicholas)	1823	Clement Moore
(Illistrations/Book)	1869	Thomas Nast
Collier Angel Cover	1898	Collier
The Christ from his Cross has vanished		Harpers Weekly
Hail Mary	1895	Olivier Merson
Nunns dressing up the crib	1880	Frank Leslies Illustrated
Clear and sweet the nuns are singing	1880	Frank Leslies Illustrated
Christmas Fairies	1900	F. A. Altwood
Santa Surprise	1894	Charles Broughton
Is OO Santy-Claus?	1898	F. A. Carter
Christmas in the South	1898	Louis Loeb
Christmas in Virginia	1871	W. L. Sheppard
A new suit	1880	Berlin Photography
Aint No Sandy Claus	1910	E. W. Kemble
Wide Awake	1872	Sol. Eytinge Jun.
Aint he a cherub	1876	Sol. Eytinge Jun.
An assisted emigrant	1895	Charles Broughton
Waiting for santa	1874	M. Woolf
In old Virginia	1894	Gilbert Gal
Light in the window	1876	M. Wood

As the author of this book I used vintage out of copyright materials, which most readers rarely get to see. In honor of these great illustrations and paintings, I have acknowledged their use for readers the opportunity to study. To hopefully one day study other great works of these illustrators.

Until 1998, renewed copyrights ran an additional 47 years. (Hence, 75 years total), rounded to the calendar year. Copyright extension bill signed in that year extended copyrights still in force an additional 20 years. Since copyrights form 1922 had already expired, anything copyrighted before 1923 is public domain in the United States, even if its copyright was renewed. Copyrights form 1923-1963, if not renewed, and not made exempt from the renewal requirements have also expired, and become public domain.

A Gilded Christmas

J. Curtis Smith